Penny™
and the magic puffballs
Roxie's First Day

BY Alonda Williams

Published 2015 by: Glori Publishing Redmond, WA 98052
www.gloripublishing.com

Publishing Contact: 908-578-9595
Printed in the United States of America

Library of Congress Control Number: 2015919495

ISBN 978-0-9912129-1-0

Penny and the Magic Puffballs - Roxie's First Day

Summary : Details the adventures of Penny, a precocious little girl who discovers the magical powers of her puffball hairstyle.

Address all inquiries to :
Alonda Williams
Email: magicpuffballs@outlook.com
For book orders visit: www.pennyandthemagicpuffballs.com or amazon.com

Cover and Interior Design by Kirk R. Myhre www.myhrecreative.com

message to parents

Penny and the magic puffballs was born out of my love for my daughter Paris, and my desire for her to feel comfortable, confident and secure in her skin. She questioned why her hair was different from all of the other girls and wondered why she couldn't wear her hair like theirs. I wanted her to know that different didn't mean bad, different was special. I also wanted to make sure that she saw main characters of color in books. So I created Penny and the magic puffballs originally as a bedtime story and decided to turn these stories into a series of books. This book is the 2nd in the Penny series and tackles issues of bullying and friendship. Girls can be mean sometimes and this story is meant to encourage readers to always be nice, especially to those who may need a friend. In this book, Penny models courage and compassion by befriending Roxie and trying to stop Bianca's bullying behavior. Bullying is everyone's business and we can all do our part to help end it. For more anti-bullying resources visit www.stopbullying.gov

 ## from Alonda

This book is dedicated to my wonderful family, Byron, Tyler and Paris. I'm so grateful God blessed me with you. I love you so much.

To Shanna, Ahlia & Ivy, thank you for being my second eyes. To Lois, Beryl, Judy and Nikki, thank you for always having my back. To little Ms. Christian, thank you so much for your creativity and for naming Roxie. Thank you to Livi and Quinn - my awesome test team.

This book is also dedicated to all of the little girls across the world who feel different. Remember different isn't bad, different is special.

 ## from Tyrus

To my wonderful clan. The ones who let daddy sit in his art office, drawing and painting for countless hours, without ever complaining. All "6 hundred" of you, Lexy, Nia, Troy, Tori and the Mighty Donovan, you guys are my favorite everything.

To my wonderful and beautiful wife Christy, thank you for letting me take this leap of faith, and allowing me to do what I've been designed to do. I love you for that.

Last but not least, thank you Alonda, for that wonderful conversation that we had, In Chicago at the Donut shop. I appreciate the belief and support. You have been a friend and a supporter, often times without saying a word. Thank you all very much.

Penny bolted out of bed. Today was going to be spectacular. It just had to be. After all, just yesterday she discovered—thanks to her mom—that her "normal" hair was not so normal at all. When her mom styled her hair in puffballs, wonderful things began to happen. These were no ordinary puffballs. They were Magic Puffballs! Yesterday, she wanted hair like everyone else, but today she loved being the only one with Magic Puffballs.

"Today will be a magical day, too. I just know it," said Penny.

4

Penny ran to find the comb and brush so her mom could freshen up her puffballs. She sat down in between her mom's knees and asked, "Mom, can you please make them puffier than ever. The puffier, the better!" Penny's mom brushed and smoothed and puffed and pulled and tugged and tucked Penny's hair until it was just perfect. Penny jumped up and rushed to the mirror. She was pleased with what she saw—two big bouncy cotton-candy puffs.

"Awesome!" Penny shouted.

Penny kissed her mom, grabbed her backpack and dashed out the door. She hopped on the school bus. She looked for a spot next to her two best friends, Grace and Symonne.

"Hi Symonne. Hi Grace. Hey—!"

Penny was surprised. Grace had a new hairstyle, which was a big deal. Grace never, ever changed her hair! She had worn her hair the same exact way- just with a different color headband- since the day Penny met her in the kindergarten sandbox.

Today, though, Grace's hair was pulled high into what looked like two big puffballs.

"Hiya, Penny," smiled Grace. "You like???"

"Yes, I love it," Penny squealed. "Absolutely love it!"

"Well, I told my mom all about your Magic Puffballs and that I absolutely, positively had to have them! I described them to my mom the best I could, and she came up with this. Not too bad, huh?? What do you think?"

"I think they are amazing!"

"So did you tell your mom about your magical day yesterday?" asked Grace.

"Of course!" said Penny. "This is the most exciting thing to happen to me in my entire lifetime. I mean, second to getting a new baby brother…and of course next to getting you two as my best friends."

"Aw, thanks!" chimed Grace and Symonne together.

"My mom said that magical things would happen whenever I wear my puffballs. She also said we all have a little magic in us. We just have to find it," declared Penny.

Grace smiled a big happy smile. "Who knows? Maybe something magical will happen to me, too."

"Yeah. Who knows, Grace?" said Penny.

When the bus pulled up to the school, a small crowd was gathered on the playground. Penny, Grace and Symonne rushed over to see what was happening. As they got closer, they saw the new girl, Roxie, surrounded by Bianca and a crowd of other girls.

Bianca was teasing Roxie.

"Why is your hair so short??? You look like a boy!" squawked Bianca, loud as ever. Roxie lowered her head, waiting for it to be over. All the other girls laughed. Roxie tried to stand strong, not responding to Bianca's badgering, but she couldn't stop her eyes from filling up with tears.

"Hey! That's not nice," said Penny, but Bianca didn't listen to her.

"Hey!" Penny exclaimed louder, but Grace and Symonne pulled her away.

"Let's not get involved," they said quietly.

Grace and Symonne felt bad for Roxie too, but they were too scared to get involved. After all, Bianca was the resident mean girl and teased and bullied everyone who dared to even breathe in her direction. They didn't want to be next. Finally, the bell rang and everyone scattered, including Bianca and her friends.

Penny, Grace and Symonne went into the building.

"Wow! It must be hard to be the new girl," said Penny.

"Yes. I bet it is," said Grace. "I've never been the new girl, but if I was I wouldn't want anyone to tease me."

"We should do something to help Roxie," declared Penny.

"Yes but what?" asked Grace.

"I don't know yet, but we can't just stand by and do nothing." Penny hoped that her Magic Puffballs would help her come up with just the right thing to do at just the right time.

The three friends started toward their class. Bianca and the other girls were in the hallway giggling. Roxie came through the playground door alone and headed straight to the bathroom. She was crying. Penny felt like running after Roxie to tell her it would be okay, but her friends ushered her into the classroom. Why was Bianca so mean?

Penny went to class and sat in her favorite seat in the cozy corner near the window next to Ivy.

"Hi, Penny," said Ivy. "Everyone has been talking about your Magic Puffballs! Are they really magic?"

"Absolutely Positively!" said Penny.

"Wow! That is so awesome," said Ivy.

"Well, Ivy, my mom says that everybody has a little magic in them.
You just have to find it."

"Hmm… even me?" asked Ivy.

"Yes, even you," declared Penny.

While Penny was excited to know that everyone was talking about
her Magic Puffballs, she couldn't stop thinking about Roxie and how
she must be feeling right now.

"Anissa?" "Present."

"Natalie?" "Here."

"Liori?" "Present."

"Julia" "I'm here."

Mrs. Bethea was taking attendance when Roxie came into the class and quietly sat in the last row. She looked like she was still crying, but she quickly wiped her eyes.

"Roxie. Is everything Okay?" Mrs. Bethea asked with concern.

"I'm okay," replied Roxie, trying to conceal her sniffles.

"Mrs. Bethea doesn't know that Roxie has a good reason for being late," thought Penny.

All morning, Penny's classmates talked about her Magic Puffballs.

"Penny, everyone is excited about your Magic Puffballs," said Anissa.

"Yeah. We all want to see if you can jump like you did yesterday," said Julia.

Penny knew that yesterday's jump rope performance was special, but she had no idea it would be one of the most talked about events in the school.

At recess, everything was different. More kids than ever headed over to the jump-rope area.

"Wow!" Penny thought, "all of this because of my Magic Puffballs!"

"Penny, we can't wait to see you jump," said Grace.

"Yeah! Do you think you can do it again?" asked Symonne.

"I know I can do it again." declared Penny as she patted her Magic Puffballs.

The crowd was getting even larger.

"Jump Pen-ny Jump! Jump Pen-ny Jump! Pen-ny!" the crowd shouted.

Penny stared at the crowd that was getting even louder. Grace and Symonne began turning the ropes.

"Come on, Penny. The whole school is waiting," said Grace.

Penny looked at all the excited faces. Everyone was cheering, waiting to see if she could break her own jump-rope record. Just yesterday, she had jumped the longest anyone had ever jumped. She felt confident and knew she could do it. But… at that very moment, the most amazing idea popped into her head. "AHA!," Penny thought, "It is easy for Bianca to pick on one person, but it would be hard for her pick on all of us.
Thanks Magic Puffballs"

As Penny looked through the crowd, she could see Roxie sitting alone on a bench on the other side of the playground. The crowd continued to shout: "Jump Pen-ny Jump! Jump Pen-ny Jump!"

Just as she was about to jump into the rope, Penny turned and ran right across the playground to the bench where Roxie was sitting. The crowd at the jump-rope area called after her:

"Penny! Penny! Where are you going? Everyone is waiting."

But Penny was already over by the bench giving Roxie a friendly wave.

"Hi. I'm Penny. Are you okay?" she asked Roxie.

"My name is Roxie. I'm new here. I'm okay, but it hurts when people tease me because my hair is different." Roxie sighed.

"Well, my hair is different, too. No one else in this school has these big ginormous puffballs, and you know what? I love them! My mom always tells me, 'Different isn't bad, different is special!'" exclaimed Penny.

"Would you like to play jump rope with us?"

Roxie paused, then she smiled and said, "Sure. I love jump rope! But I'm not very good."

"That's okay," declared Penny. "My magic puffballs will take care of that."

Penny and a puzzled Roxie walked back over to the jump-rope area together.

"Hey everybody. This is my new friend Roxie, and she loves to play jump rope, too."

"Hi Roxie!"

Grace and Symonne picked up the rope. "Okay! Let's do this!" they shouted and started turning the rope again.

"Okay, magic puffballs do your thing," thought Penny.

Roxie jumped in first, then Penny followed, and the two new friends jumped together. Everyone started to count—1, 2, 3 4—Roxie and Penny jumped and jumped—10, 11, 12, 13—all the way to 100. Everyone clapped, even Bianca clapped reluctantly and Roxie smiled from ear to ear. She couldn't believe how well she was jumping. Penny didn't break her jump-rope record, but jumping with Roxie was so much better.

All the other kids came over to meet Roxie.

"How did you learn to jump so well?" asked Grace.

"I don't know. I used to jump rope at my old school, but I was never that good."

Penny knew there was only one explanation for this. "Of course this was the work of my magic and wonderful puffballs," she confirmed.

"Are your puffballs really magic?" Roxie asked quizzically.

"Absolutely, positively," confirmed Penny.

On the bus ride home, Grace was a little sad.

"What's wrong, Grace?" asked Penny.

"Well, I was so looking forward to some sort of magic coming from my puffballs. I guess mine aren't so magical after all."

"Grace, not everyone can have Magic Puffballs. You have to find out what your magic is. Besides, I think making a new friend is pretty magical," said Penny.

"Yes, I guess you are right," sighed Grace, feeling a little better.

"Maybe Bianca won't bother Roxie anymore because now she has so many friends. That would be pretty magical to me said Symonne.

"Maybe so, but I think we should tell the teacher anyway. Just in case," chimed Penny.

That night, as Penny was getting ready for bed, she told her mom all about Roxie, Bianca, and what had happened at school.

"Mom, Bianca was being so mean to Roxie. All because of her hair."

"Penny," Mom soothed, "sometimes people are mean, and we don't understand why. What's important is that you did an amazing thing today. You were brave and kind and made someone else feel great. I am so proud of you." Penny's mom snuggled her and kissed her on the forehead.

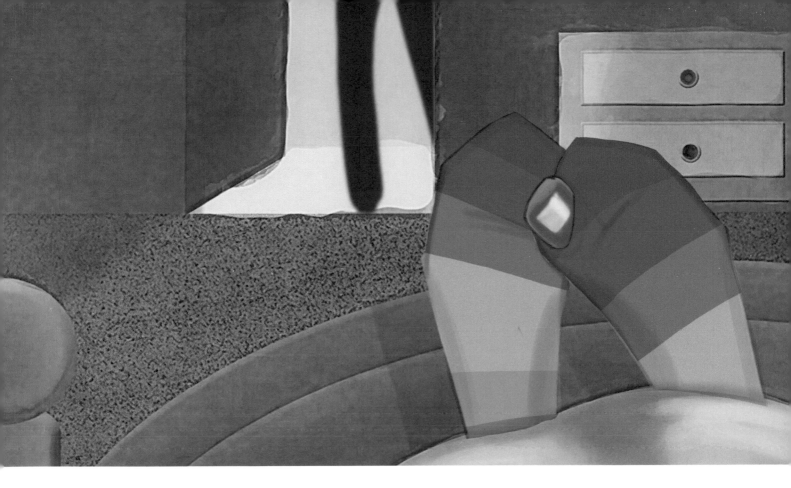

"Thanks, Mom. I'm glad I made friends with Roxie. She is really nice."

"I met Roxie's mom at the PTA meeting, and she told me all about her. Roxie is a special little girl who has been sick for a long time. Sometimes she needs to take medicine that makes her hair fall out. It's just starting to grow back. Penny's mom spoke gently.

Wow!" Penny was shocked to hear that Roxie was sick. "I guess you never know what's going on with someone."

"That's right, Penny. That's why it's always best just to be nice."

Penny lay in her bed thinking about her day. She was so happy that she and her Magic Puffballs helped Roxie have a magical day. She was excited about making every day just as magical. She closed her eyes, snuggled under the covers and wondered what would happen tomorrow and the next day . Wonderful adventures were in store for Penny and her ~~puffballs.~~

Magic Puffballs!

power

CPSIA information can be obtained at www.ICGtesting.com
Printed in the USA
LVIW011712300819
629373LV00015BA/217